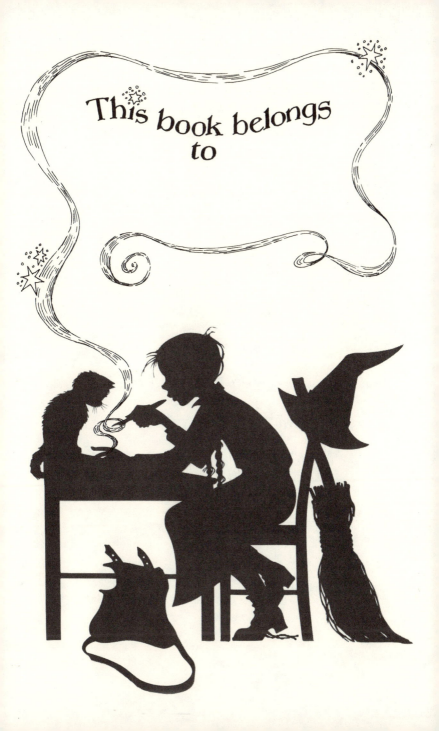

This book belongs
to

The Magical Adventures of
The Worst Witch

The Worst Witch

The Worst Witch Strikes Again

A Bad Spell for the Worst Witch

The Worst Witch at Sea

The Worst Witch Saves the Day

The Worst Witch to the Rescue

The Worst Witch and the Wishing Star

First Prize for the Worst Witch

FIRST PRIZE
FOR
THE WORST WITCH

JILL MURPHY

CANDLEWICK PRESS

First U.S. edition 2020

Library of Congress Catalog Card Number pending
ISBN 978-1-5362-1101-6

20 21 22 23 24 25 LBM 10 9 8 7 6 5 4 3 2 1

Printed in Melrose Park, IL, U.S.A.

This book was typeset in Baskerville.
The illustrations were done in ink.

Candlewick Press
99 Dover Street
Somerville, Massachusetts 02144

visit us at www.candlewick.com

For Pamela Todd
with tons of Love

'What Larks eh?'

CHAPTER ONE

MILDRED HUBBLE was cruising above the trees and villages on her way to Miss Cackle's Academy for the start of Summer Term. Like all her classmates, she was longing to get this last term over with and go up to the very top class next year, when they would be the proud wearers of the Year-Five uniform to set them apart from the lower school. In fact, there was not much difference to the usual uniform, only a multi-striped tie and braid sewn round their cloaks, but Year Four couldn't wait to be wearing it.

There seemed to be more luggage with each passing term, especially *this* one, Mildred reflected as she peered down through the treetops, looking out for the usual landmarks. Apart from her bags of clothes and books; her cat, Tabby; and her tortoise, Einstein (both tucked up safely in the cat basket), there was also Star, the stray dog she had found last term. Star had proved to be such a natural acrobat that he and Mildred had won the national swimming-pool competition for Miss Cackle's Academy. After such a triumph Mildred had been allowed to keep him as her broom companion.

Star was perched behind Mildred on top of a box of books, as if it was the most natural place in the world for him to sit, and every now and then he let out a volley of barks, which made Mildred feel as if he was talking to her.

"Come on, Star!" Mildred called back to him. "You can sit at the front with me if you like. We'll be flying for at least another hour—we've only just passed over the water mill at Greater Bustling."

Star leapt over her shoulder in an instant, landing neatly in her lap.

"Woof!" he barked, giving her a joyful slurp under the chin.

"Oh, look!" exclaimed Mildred. "There's a big striped tent down there at the edge of the village—it must be a circus! What a shame it's so far from the school or we could have pleaded with Miss Cackle to take us there for an outing."

As she said this, Star took a flying leap back over her shoulder and dived between the book box and the cat basket.

"Hey!" said Mildred. "What's the matter, boy? Is it a bit too windy for you up this high? Come on — let's fly a bit lower down."

A blustery wind had sprung up, and the broomstick was swaying from side to side and making sudden lurches, hindered by the luggage piled on top and hanging from the back of it.

Mildred dropped down six metres, hovering evenly like a helicopter.

"There you are," she said to Star. "That's *much* better — hardly any wind at all. You can jump back if you like."

However, to Mildred's surprise, he didn't move from his hideaway, and no amount of cajoling, even the offer of a treat, could tempt him out.

Twenty minutes passed and Mildred still hadn't seen anyone from the academy. She was just beginning to wonder if she'd got the wrong day when, to her great relief, she saw Maud flying along steadily in front of her.

"Maud! Maudie!" she yelled, delighted
to see her best friend. "What a fantastic bit
of luck! You're the first Cackle-ite I've seen
this morning."

"Millie!" squealed Maud, equally thrilled.

They tried to fling their arms round each
other but gave up, laughing as they clashed
broomsticks and narrowly avoided falling
off.

"Concentrate, girls!" bellowed Mildred
sternly, doing an excellent impression of

Miss Hardbroom, the strictest teacher in the school. *"I don't expect to see such silly nonsense from fourth-years!"*

"Gosh, Mildred," said Maud, "you sound scarily like her. I wonder what ghastly projects she's lined up for us this term."

"Well, one thing's for sure," said Mildred. "There's going to be a lot of swimming!"

"Oh yes, of course! I'd forgotten about the swimming pool," said Maud. "Do you think they've actually built it yet?"

"I don't know," said Mildred, "but I had a crash course of swimming lessons during the hols just in case."

"I didn't know you couldn't swim," said Maud. "You managed all right when we went on holiday to Grim Cove."

Mildred smiled. "I just pretended," she confessed. "I hopped along on one foot and did swimming movements—I didn't want Ethel sneering!"

Over the years Ethel had somehow become an implacable enemy of Mildred and never missed an opportunity to make her look small.

"Well, no one noticed," said Maud.

"And now they never will!" said Mildred. "I can do ten lengths of our local pool, which is huge. The school pool will be a quarter of that size, so it should be fine."

"It's going to be brilliant," said Maud happily. "Lovely, warm, clear water, with sparkly blue tiles—and all thanks to Mildred Hubble and Star! Where is he, by the way? He's too big to go in the cat basket."

"He's hiding in between the luggage," said Mildred. "I don't think he's feeling too well. He was fine when we started out—I probably shouldn't have given him any breakfast."

CHAPTER TWO

ON THE LAST day of Summer Term there was a ceremony called Fourth-Year Firsts, when prizes were awarded to pupils who had proved themselves best in certain subjects over the past four years. It was also the occasion when the witch chosen to be Head Girl for the coming year would be solemnly announced. This event was actually more important to the girls than the final year itself, when there would be no time for distractions, as everyone would be working madly to pass the Witches' Higher Certificate.

"Have you got any hopes for Fourth-Year Firsts?" asked Maud, passing Mildred a chocolate biscuit as they coasted along smoothly, cloaks and hair streaming behind them in the wind.

"Not *exactly*," replied Mildred. "What about you? Tell me yours and then I'll tell you mine."

"Well," said Maud, "I'm sort of average at everything, but there *is* a First Prize for Team Spirit, so I'm going to work on that one — you know, being extra helpful and so on. What about you?"

"If I tell you what I'd like to get," confided Mildred, smiling shyly at her friend, "you have to promise not to laugh."

"Cross my heart!" promised Maud.

"OK then," said Mildred. "It isn't *exactly* a first prize, more of an honour, but it would be the only first prize that I would want."

"Go on!" urged Maud, intrigued. "Tell me!"

"You mustn't laugh!" Mildred reminded her.

"My word is my bond," said Maud, looking at Mildred with a very serious face.

"Right," announced Mildred. "I'd like to be chosen as Head Girl for next year."

Maud really did try to keep her serious face on, but almost immediately she erupted into such peals of laughter that she nearly fell off her broom.

"You promised not to laugh!" exclaimed Mildred indignantly. However, within seconds she was drawn into Maud's infectious and unstoppable fit of giggles, and soon the two of them were doubled over on their broomsticks, desperately trying to steer and keep their balance.

"It isn't *that* funny!" snorted Mildred. "I have done quite a few good things for the school, in between disasters!"

Maud was now laughing so much that tears streamed down her cheeks and blew away in the wind. "Sorry, Mil!" she howled. "It's just so incredibly un*likely*."

"Understatement of the year!" Mildred laughed, beginning to wonder why she had ever mentioned it in the first place.

"And anyway," continued Maud, between fits of mirth, "if there's a Hallow in the school, it always goes to them, and we've got Ethel Hallow——"

"*Un*fortunately!" commented Mildred.

For some reason, this observation struck them both as so utterly hilarious that they could hardly see——what with their screwed-up faces and their tears of laughter and the buffeting wind — and they suddenly realized that the treetops were alarmingly close.

"Come on, Mil!" said Maud, trying hard to calm down. "Let's land in that nice big field down there and take a ten-minute break before we have a crash landing."

"Good idea, Maudie," agreed Mildred, explosions of laughter still erupting every few seconds. "I must say, there really is *nothing* quite like a good fit of the giggles!"

CHAPTER THREE

ETHEL HALLOW, an hour ahead of Mildred and Maud, was flying very fast at a high altitude, baggage jolting behind her; even her perfect cat, Nightstar, was having difficulty holding on. Ethel's best friend, Drusilla, who was not such an accomplished flier as Ethel, was trying frantically to keep up. Ethel was in a *very* bad mood,

remembering how Mildred Hubble had somehow managed to drag herself up from total hopelessness to become quite an exceptional pilot, with that scruffy little rescue dog as her broom companion.

"*Please* slow down, Ethel!" yelled Drusilla, doing her best to keep the annoyance out of her voice, as it always made things worse if you tried to stand up to Ethel. "I'm going to fall off in a minute! We aren't all

brilliant fliers like you," she added, hoping that flattery might improve things.

It did. Ethel slowed to a calmer speed, and they both turned round to check that their luggage was secure and to reassure their ruffled cats. Nightstar, who had a rather touchy temperament like his owner, turned his back on Ethel, stuck one leg in the air, and began washing. He wasn't the sort of cat to let on that he had been scared.

"What is it, Eth?" asked Drusilla. "You were OK five minutes ago."

"I was just thinking about Mildred Hubble," replied Ethel grumpily. "I mean, how on earth has she actually got through four years at Cackle's? Every time she messes something up, I think, 'Bingo! That's got rid of her!' Then she somehow manages to make things better for herself, and now that she has that ridiculous dog on her broomstick, she's actually turned into a really decent flier. If she was still with that awful cat, she'd be back to square one just like that." She clicked her fingers. "It *so* isn't fair. I mean, she might even win First Prize for Best Pilot at this rate, especially now that they've won the swimming-pool competition together and everyone thinks they're *so* perfect."

18

"Don't get in a state about it, Ethel," said Drusilla soothingly. "You'll definitely win First Prize for Chanting *and* for Potions. Mildred's hopeless at both."

"I'm not *in* a state, thank you very much, Drusilla," snarled Ethel dangerously. "And she *isn't* actually hopeless at potions anymore, thanks to that animal-speaking spell she invented last year that got me into so much trouble."

"Ethel!" exclaimed Drusilla before she could stop herself. "You really can't blame Mildred for what happened! You *did* steal her spell and pretend it was yours."

"Look, Drusilla," snapped Ethel, "whose side are you on? Why don't you go and team up with Mildred's little gang of friends if you think they're so great?"

"Sorry, Ethel," mumbled Drusilla miserably. "Of course I'm on your side— always, whatever happens. Anyway, one thing you can be sure of: you'll definitely be announced as Head Girl for next year! If there's a Hallow in the running, they always get elected — there have been at least thirty-five Hallow Head Girls over the centuries."

"Yes, at least that's a sure thing," agreed Ethel moodily.

In the distance, they could see the shadowy shape of Miss Cackle's Academy for Witches perched on top of a mountain, half-hidden among dense pine trees. Already, other pupils were visible on the horizon, struggling with their baggage and cat baskets.

"Come on, Druse," said Ethel, feeling a little better at the thought of the gold Head-Girl medal, pinned weightily to her multicoloured Year-Five tie. "We'd better get a move on if we're going to arrive before anyone else — First Prize for Perfect Punctuality as well as everything else!"

"We hope!" Drusilla laughed, relieved that they were friends again.

Ethel suddenly took off with such a whoosh of air that Drusilla's hat flew off

20

and spiralled into the trees below.

"Hang on a mo!" called Drusilla, but Ethel was already too far ahead to hear her. It was a very pleasant morning, Ethel reflected as the school grew closer, turrets glinting in the early-morning sun and the vast beech forest beginning to mingle with the dark pines that surrounded the school.

"Nearly there, Druse," she shouted over her shoulder. "Druse?"

She turned and saw her friend far behind her, desperately trying to catch up. Ethel could just make out her voice in between gusts of wind.

"Ethel, wait!" she was calling. "*Please* wait! I've found something really interesting!"

Ethel hovered impatiently.

"Come on, Drusilla," she snapped. "What have you been *doing* back there? We're going to be *last* at this rate."

"Sorry, Ethel," said Drusilla, juddering to an untidy halt. "I dropped my hat — but while I was down in the forest looking for it, I found this pinned to a tree. Take a look!" She handed Ethel a small, faded poster.

Ethel smoothed out the poster on her lap. "I don't believe it!" she exclaimed when she saw what was on it. "Gosh, Druse, what an amazing bit of luck on the first day of term — especially after what we were talking about!"

"What shall we do with it?" asked Drusilla.

"I think we'd better take it to Miss Cackle," said Ethel, a horrible smile creeping across her face. "I mean, it's our *duty*, really, isn't it?"

CHAPTER FOUR

IN THE PLAYGROUND there was the usual mixture of teachers keeping a beady eye on the arrivals: new pupils anxiously trying to land successfully and old friends joyously reuniting.

"Look, Maud," said Mildred. "There's Enid!"

"Hey, you two!" shouted their friend, leaving her broomstick hovering and rushing to greet them with a delighted hug.

"Quick," said Maud. "We'd better line up—they're here!"

Miss Hardbroom and Miss Cackle had suddenly appeared, quite literally, in the middle of the playground.

Miss Hardbroom clapped her hands. "Line up now, girls," she commanded, already sounding slightly irritated even though no one had done anything wrong. "Hurry along. You all know the drill."

Everyone hastened into line, arranging their assortment of luggage and broomsticks in neat rows beside them.

"Excellent, girls!" Miss Cackle smiled with all the warmth that her terrifying deputy lacked. "Wonderful to see you all looking so cheerful and rested after your nice long holiday."

"Brains fully recharged and ready for lots of hard work, I hope!" Miss Hardbroom cut in grimly.

"But of course, Miss Hardbroom," twittered Miss Cackle. "Now then, girls, I expect you all want to know about the swimming pool! Well, it was finished just in time for the start of term and is up and running. So I thought, as Mildred's form won the pool for us, that they could have first dip, as it were!"

Mildred's class let out cries of joy, and Mildred and Enid actually jumped up and down, but only for a few seconds as Miss Hardbroom shot them a glance that quenched any high spirits like a water cannon.

Miss Drill, who was Form Four's teacher, also flashed a look at the girls, but hers was full of pride and happiness.

After everyone had parked their broomsticks in the broom shed, Miss Drill announced that Form Four could collect their swimming costumes and towels as soon as they'd unpacked and meet at the new pool in the old Small Playground, a yard that had originally been used for individual broomstick lessons.

"This is just brilliant!" exclaimed Maud as she joined the bustling throng of excited pupils making their way through the maze of corridors.

"It's along here," said Mildred cheerfully. "I've had lots of extra lessons there over the years, so I remember exactly where it is!"

"I expect you do," came Ethel's sneering tones. "Of course, *I've* never been there in

my life, as I could already fly like a profess-
ional by the time I was three years old!"

"You get younger every time you mention
your early flying skills," Maud replied
witheringly over her shoulder. "Sure it
wasn't three months?"

"Anyway," said Enid loyally, "Mildred's
one of our best fliers now, so all those extra
lessons must have paid off."

"True," agreed Ethel with a wink at
Drusilla, "but only because she found that
stupid dog."

"Oh, do lay off," said Maud. "Can't you
just be nice for five minutes, Ethel? We've
got swimming as our first lesson of term,
thanks to Mildred."

"Yes — and she's as good a pilot as anyone
now," said Enid, "*and* Miss Cackle said she
can keep the dog forever, so nothing's going
to change."

"I wouldn't be quite so sure of that,"
mumbled Ethel to Drusilla, so quietly that
no one else heard.

"Here it is!" yelled Mildred from the front of the line. They all stopped to look at the new door with SWIMMING POOL emblazoned across it. Apart from the gold lettering, it was the usual type of sturdy wooden door, and for a brief moment, Mildred wondered if there really was a swimming pool on the other side.

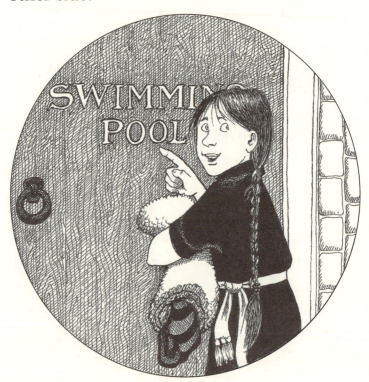

CHAPTER FIVE

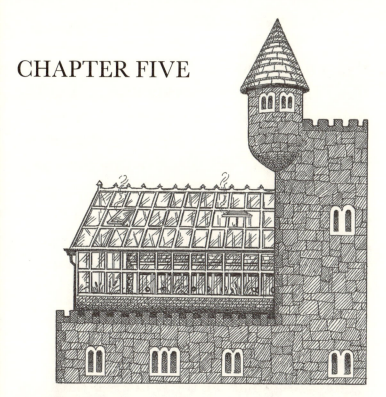

THERE WAS indeed a swimming pool—but it was not quite what the girls had been expecting. True, it was a large rectangle full of water, but the structure surrounding it was like an enormous old-fashioned greenhouse, with a huge pitched roof made entirely of steel struts and glass. Several of the skylights were propped open to let out the condensation, but they also let in the wind that whipped constantly around the high castle walls, and the girls shivered as they imagined getting into their costumes.

Neat rows of changing rooms ran along one side of the pool, but there were huge gaps at the top and bottom of the doors, so there would be no escape from the cold. To make matters worse, the water was so crammed with bulrushes and plants that no one could quite imagine how they would actually get in and attempt any sort of swimming. Far from the turquoise tiles of Maud's imagination, the water was dark and sinister; you couldn't see the bottom, and it looked as though *things* might be lurking.

Miss Hardbroom and Miss Drill stood at the far end of the pool, watching as Form Four shuffled through the door, keeping close together like a huddle of penguins contemplating a snowstorm.

"This is an ecological pool," explained Miss Hardbroom. "Self-cleaning, with

carefully chosen plants, so no need for chlorine or any polluting chemicals, which means it's full of fascinating pond life—perfect for your natural history studies, which you can get on with while you're taking exercise. There you are, girls, two lessons together—an excellent use of time management and brain power! Any questions before you all get 'stuck in,' as they say nowadays?"

The girls saw the flicker of amusement flitting momentarily across Miss Hardbroom's stern features as she noted the appalled expressions on their faces.

"What *sort* of pond life is in the pool, Miss Hardbroom?" asked Mildred nervously.

"Many wonderful creatures," replied Miss Hardbroom. "There are water snails to assist with the cleaning process; all sorts of flying insects, which will find their way in and out of the skylights; frogs, of course; and dragonflies. Their underwater larvae have an extraordinary hinged lower lip, which they use to *grab* their prey and deliver it into their crushing mandibles—"

"What are mandibles?" whispered Enid to Mildred.

"Look it up later, Enid," Miss Hardbroom interjected seamlessly. "Plus lots of healthy silt at the bottom to assist with frog spawn and other developing larvae and eggs."

The girls remained in their huddle, transfixed with horror at the thought of plunging into the uninviting brown, cloudy water. They were also wondering how Miss Hardbroom had managed to hear Enid's whisper from ten metres away. Although they had been at the school for four years now, it never failed to surprise them when Miss Hardbroom seemed to pick up every-thing they said, even if she wasn't actually in the room. Sometimes she seemed to know what they were thinking, which made life extremely nerve-racking for Mildred, who was often hatching a plan that she would rather keep secret.

CHAPTER SIX

THE NEXT morning, Mildred and Maud were perched on chairs outside Miss Cackle's study. During breakfast one of the first-years had been sent to find Mildred with a message that Miss Cackle wanted to see her. Mildred was convinced that she must be in some sort of trouble, so Maud was waiting with her until she went in.

"Don't worry, Mil," soothed Maud, patting her friend's arm. "You know that you haven't put a foot wrong—"

"Yet," added Mildred gloomily.

"We only arrived yesterday!" Maud laughed. "She's probably just going to ask you to run some errand, or maybe she's going to give you a special award for winning the pool in the first place."

"Or perhaps she's going to ask me to be Head Girl next year!" said Mildred with a smile. "We could always look on the bright side!"

"ENTER!" called Miss Cackle.

Mildred and Maud leapt to their feet.

"I'll be here when you come out," said Maud, grabbing Mildred for one last hug.

Mildred found herself sitting across the desk from Miss Cackle and Miss Hardbroom.

36

"Good morning, Mildred, my dear," said Miss Cackle in a kind voice.

"Good morning, Miss Cackle," answered Mildred. "Good morning, Miss Hardbroom."

"And good morning to you too, Mildred," replied Miss Hardbroom, sounding slightly friendly.

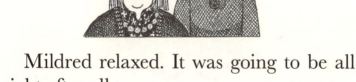

Mildred relaxed. It was going to be all right after all.

"Well now," continued Miss Cackle, "I expect you must be wondering why I sent for you."

"I *was*, rather," replied Mildred humbly.

"Let's not beat about the bush, Miss Cackle," said Miss Hardbroom.

"Quite right, Miss Hardbroom," agreed

Miss Cackle. "Here, Mildred—we think you should take a look at this."

She pushed a tattered piece of paper across the desk, and Mildred could see at once that it was a lost dog poster. The poster was faded, but clear enough to show a ringmaster in a top hat, a lady on a trapeze, a seal, and a Shetland pony. Sitting on the back of the pony was a small dog.

"It's Star!" gasped Mildred.

"Yes," said Miss Cackle. "I'm afraid it is. Drusilla found this poster in the forest yesterday and Ethel thought I ought to see it. Well, we always did wonder where he'd come from, didn't we?"

"And now we know," said Miss Hardbroom.

"But it's a circus," said Mildred, "so it must have moved on by now. Look, the poster is really faded, so it's been there for ages. They're probably hundreds of miles away—" She stopped abruptly, remembering the circus tent she had flown over at Greater Bustling, which was only twenty miles from the school. "He's so happy with me now," she blurted out, "*and* he helps me to fly. I can't give him back. *Please,* Miss Cackle, can we just not tell anyone? They've probably got another dog by now anyway. *Please!*"

She began to cry, huge tears sliding down her face, while trying hard to control herself, as she could see from Miss Hardbroom's pursed lips that getting hysterical wouldn't help.

"This *is* a very difficult situation, Mildred," said Miss Hardbroom, sounding faintly sympathetic, which gave Mildred a glimmer of hope, "and we *can* see your point of view, but if the dog actually belongs to"—she glanced at the poster with distaste before continuing—"Brilliantine's Amazing Travelling Circus, we ought at least to find out if they want him back. No wonder he had such a fine sense of balance—just look at him on the back of that pony."

Mildred gazed at both teachers, utter desperation written across her face, hoping she could will them into changing their minds.

"That's everything we know so far," said Miss Cackle. "Don't look so tragic, my dear. Perhaps we won't be able to find the circus after all—then you'll be able to keep the little acrobat, and at least we will know that we've tried to do the right thing."

"That will be all for the present,

Mildred," said Miss Hardbroom, sensing that the kindly headmistress could prattle on for another ten minutes, eating into her potions time with the Year Threes.

Mildred dragged herself out of the room, feeling as if a lead-lined cloak had been dropped over her shoulders.

"What on earth has happened, Millie?" asked Maud as Mildred fell sobbing into her arms.

"It's Star," said Mildred. "He was lost from a circus and they're trying to find it and give him back — and it's all Ethel's fault! Why does she always have to ruin everything for me?"

CHAPTER SEVEN

MILDRED sat hunched on her bed, wearing Tabby round her neck and clasping Star tightly in her arms. He was so delighted to have Mildred's company mid-morning that he didn't notice her tears falling onto his fur. It was break time, and the three friends had sneaked up to Mildred's room to make a plan to keep him.

"It's probably all going to be a storm in a teacup," said Maud. "I'm sure they'll never be able to find the circus anyway."

"Oh, yes they will," muttered Mildred. "Ethel's probably hiring a detective right now."

"Well, I think Maud's right," said Enid. "H.B. and Miss Cackle are *far* too busy bossing us all around to waste time zooming up and down the country looking for a travelling circus."

"The thing is," said Mildred, "it *hasn't* travelled that far. I saw the tent on the edge of Greater Bustling as I flew into school yesterday, and that's only twenty miles away."

"Are you sure it's the same one?" asked Enid hopefully. "Perhaps it was just a tent—you know, like the ones people use for parties?"

Mildred shook her head. "No," she replied gloomily. "It was definitely a big striped circus tent, and now come to think of it, Star hid behind me when he saw it as we were flying over. You see, he doesn't want to go back, and it would be cruel to make him."

"I think we'd do best to keep quiet about it," said Maud, "and, whatever you do, don't say anything to Ethel."

"Why not?" asked Mildred. "I was going to tell her exactly what I think of her."

"Well," said Maud wisely, "if Miss Cackle and H.B. *don't* make a huge effort to find the circus, enough time might pass so that they genuinely give up, and Star will be safe with you. If you start an argument with Ethel, it will fire her up to find the circus, just to make things worse for you."

"Thanks, Maudie," said Mildred, smiling gratefully at her friend. "You always know what to do."

CHAPTER EIGHT

THERE WERE so many things to occupy every waking moment that Year Four were often falling asleep over their dinner by the end of each day. Mildred actually began to forget about the circus for most of the time, as they concentrated on swimming sessions twice a week, double lessons of chanting, and broomstick aerobatics, while grappling with several complicated new spells.

One of their favourites was a spell to turn any sort of brush into a flying object. This was a Privilege Spell given to the Form Four pupils in preparation for their final year. Until now, the pupils had used broomsticks, which were already primed to fly, so it was most exciting to enchant flying objects of their choice.

It took two days of learning chants and working out sizing, similar to the animal-speaking spell that Mildred had invented, for which you had to get the measurements correct before the spell would work.

Once they'd finally mastered the spell, Mildred, Maud, and Enid had great fun in Mildred's room during break time, enchanting a motley selection of anything with bristles attached, just for fun. Maud persuaded a snail to perch on a toothbrush and kept the brush very steady while it flew sedately across the room. The snail didn't seem to mind at all and carried on gliding up the plastic handle without a care in the world.

Enid had chosen a dustpan and brush, and she was delighted when they both took off together, as she had cast the spell when the brush was resting inside the dustpan. The brush chased the pan around the room, skimming the ceiling, and even tried to sweep the bats off the picture rail, causing great upset as they were trying to have their daytime sleep. The brush seemed to have a life of its own, and in the end Enid had to rugby-tackle it, while Maud grabbed the dustpan and held on to it tightly until it had calmed down.

Mildred chose a hairbrush, with Enid's hamster Nibbles (Enid had been hiding him in her room) balanced on top. She did her best to keep the hairbrush level, but the hamster hated it and clung on with his eyes shut, looking as if he had taken lessons from Tabby.

"Take him off, Millie!" said Enid, laughing. "He really hates it. Give him to me and I'll put him back in my room."

Mildred and Maud tidied away their flying implements and curled up on the bed for a chat. There were no chairs in their cramped rooms, so it was either the bed or the floor.

"It's gone very quiet on the circus-finding front," confided Mildred. "Nobody's mentioned it again, so maybe they've given up."

"Given up what?" asked Enid, returning from her room, where she had put the traumatized Nibbles back under her bed.

"Mildred was just saying maybe H.B. and Miss Cackle have given up trying to find the circus," said Maud, "so it's looking hopeful for Star."

"It *does* seem hopeful," agreed Enid. "The poster was found in the beech forest just below our mountain, so the circus must have been near here and then moved on in the opposite direction until it got to Greater Bustling. Mildred saw it there on her way to school, so let's just hope it's gone on another twenty miles by now."

"Or maybe sixty!" said Maud.

Mildred laughed. "Why stop at sixty?

Let's make it three hundred miles and falling into the sea!"

Unfortunately, Drusilla was outside the door to Mildred's room, listening to this conversation. She had been feeling guilty about finding the poster and giving it to Ethel, especially as everyone now knew that Mildred was upset, which had made Drusilla unpopular with the rest of the class. As usual, Ethel had somehow managed to hide the fact that she was the one who had taken the poster to Miss Cackle.

Ethel was such a difficult person to be best friends with, reflected Drusilla, and she was very grumpy at the moment, as nothing had come of her attempt to sabotage Mildred's flying skills by getting rid of Star.

Drusilla had been on the verge of apologizing to Mildred for giving the poster to Ethel in the first place, but, as she pressed her ear to the door and heard the vital piece of information about the whereabouts of the circus, the weak side of her nature over-rode the impulse to be kind.

She knew that it would please Ethel to get rid of Mildred's dog, and Drusilla found herself imagining how nice her difficult friend would be — at least for a day or two.

She couldn't resist it, and turning away from the door, she went to find Ethel.

CHAPTER NINE

YEAR FOUR WERE out in the playground having a flying lesson with Miss Drill. They had been allowed to try out their brush-enchantment spells, and everyone (even Mildred) had got their calculations spot on.

The playground was full of gleeful girls casting spells and trundling along on an assortment of normal household brooms and yard brooms. Enid had managed to find a feather duster with a long handle and was hunched over with her feet almost touching the ground. Her cat was hanging on while trying to catch the feathers, and the girls were helpless with laughter, watching as they bobbed along. Even Miss Drill couldn't resist smiling.

"*Very* funny, Enid," she said, trying (and failing) to look stern. "But I think a feather duster isn't *quite* the thing, is it? Off you hop and find something else. There are still a few household brooms in the corner to choose from."

The door from the school opened and an anxious-looking first-year came out and handed a note to Miss Drill. The girl was so nervous that she actually curtsied, and the pupils all burst out laughing.

"Thank you, Dulcie," said Miss Drill. "No need to curtsy, dear — I'm not the queen. That will be all now. Off you go."

Dulcie couldn't stop herself curtsying again, amid gales of laughter.

Miss Drill read the contents of the note. "Now then," she said, "I need Mildred Hubble for a moment. Miss Cackle and Miss Hardbroom want to see you in the headmistress's study immediately. Don't forget to deactivate your yard broom before you go; otherwise anyone could make it fly—Oh, and it's all right to take Star with you. It says so in the note."

"Thank you, Miss Drill," replied Mildred, jumping off the broom and deactivating it before putting it back on the pile.

"I wonder what they want," whispered Maud to Enid.

"No idea," said Enid, who was measuring Mildred's yard broom to try to work out the size part of the spell. "But I'm sure we'll soon find out."

CHAPTER TEN

AS THEY approached Miss Cackle's study, Star had begun sniffing the ground like a bloodhound until he arrived at the gap beneath the door. He took one last sniff, jerked the lead out of Mildred's hand, and trotted off determinedly down the corridor.

"Star!" called Mildred. "Come back here!" But, to her great surprise, he took no notice at all and disappeared round the corner.

"ENTER!" called Miss Hardbroom's voice, sounding as sharp and unwelcoming as ever, leaving Mildred no choice but to go in without him.

There, inside the headmistress's study, was Mildred's worst nightmare come true. Miss Cackle was busy handing cups of tea to a man and a woman who were dressed in rather gaudy clothes—although most people looked gaudy compared to the staff and girls at Miss Cackle's Academy.

The woman was wearing a pink hat with a flower on it and a striped poncho, and the man had a bushy mustache and a bright red jacket. Even without the ringmaster's outfit and the woman's trapeze costume from the poster, Mildred knew exactly who they were.

"Ah, Mildred," said Miss Cackle. "Come and sit down. Mr. and Mrs. Brilliantine, this is Mildred Hubble, who found your lost dog and has been taking excellent care of him for you. Mildred, this is Mr. and Mrs. Brilliantine, owners of the circus that we've been attempting to find, as you know."

"Where *is* the dog, Mildred?" asked Miss Hardbroom.

"He ran off down the corridor," replied Mildred. "Shall I go and find him?"

"In a moment, my dear," said Miss Cackle in her warmest voice. "I'm sure he won't have gone far—would you like a macaroon?"

"No thank you, Miss Cackle," said Mildred in a very small voice.

"While you all chat," said Miss Hardbroom, "I'll go and check the corridor to Mildred's room; he's probably up there somewhere."

Mr. and Mrs. Brilliantine were surprisingly nice and thoughtful. Miss Cackle had already explained to them how attached Mildred and the dog had become— Mildred had perked up on hearing this— but her hopes were dashed when Miss Cackle told them that Mildred had always known he would have to go back to the circus if it was found.

Mrs. Brilliantine leaned forward and patted Mildred's hand.

"I can see how upset you must feel about this, my dear," she said kindly, "but we have so missed him at our little circus. It really is very small, and he was always the best thing in it. He fell out of the back of his crate while we were on the move and got hopelessly lost."

"I'm not going to lie to you," said Mr. Brilliantine. "It wasn't an easy life for him in the circus. Between shows, he was in his crate most of the time, but he got plenty of food, and the audience loved him."

"Audiences are hard to come by these days," said Mrs. Brilliantine, "so we really would like him back, if you could bear to part with him."

Hope flared in Mildred's heart.

"Well, I'd rather *not*—" she began.

"Of course she can," said Miss Cackle. "He wasn't hers in the first place, was he, Mildred? Just on loan. Ah, there he is now."

They heard Star before the door opened, and Miss Hardbroom came in holding him in a vise-like grip as he yelped and struggled.

"BINKY!" exclaimed Mrs. Brilliantine. "Come to Mummy!"

"That's him, all right!" agreed Mr. Brilliantine. "Full of beans, as ever. Come here, old chap."

Miss Hardbroom put the dog down on the floor and dragged him, all four feet splayed, past Mildred to his rightful owners. He gave a despairing glance at Mildred, who realized that there was nothing she could do to stop it. He would have to be returned to these people whether she liked it or not.

Mildred stood up and took his lead. "Come on now, Star—I mean Binky," she said, kneeling and trying to keep the quaver out of her voice. "It's time to go home. We've had such fun, haven't we? I won't forget you."

She looked up at Miss Cackle. "Can I visit sometimes, once he's settled back in?"

"I *don't* think so, Mildred," said Miss Hardbroom before the Brilliantines could respond. "That would just confuse him—and you. Best to make a clean break, don't you agree, Miss Cackle?"

"I rather think Miss Hardbroom is right, Mildred," said the headmistress.

As Mildred handed the lead to Mrs. Brilliantine, Star sat down suddenly and drooped, as if he had completely given up. He wouldn't look at Mildred and kept his head lowered, still as a mouse with an owl hovering overhead.

Mildred thought she might explode trying to keep the tears at bay.

Meanwhile, Mr. Brilliantine had been peering around the room, taking in the strange outfits worn by Miss Cackle and Miss Hardbroom.

"What sort of school *is* this?" he asked rather suddenly.

"Difficult to describe, really," replied Miss Cackle with a smile.

"It's very old-fashioned," said Miss Hardbroom crisply. "Old-style values and extremely hardworking."

"But lots of fun too," added Miss Cackle. "A *magic* sort of school, you might say! Off you go now, Mildred—you've done very well. I'm sure the dog will be fine once he's settled back into his old home."

"Yes, Miss Cackle. Thank you, Miss Cackle," said Mildred, and she left the room without looking back even once, as she was kind enough not to make things worse for the little dog when there really was nothing she could do to stop them taking him away.

Mildred went straight to her room, and that's where Maud and Enid found her, under the covers with Tabby, sobbing her heart out.

"What is it, Mil?" exclaimed Maud, perching on the edge of the bed, trying to get an arm round her.

"It's Star," wept Mildred, sitting up with Tabby still clutched tightly to her chest. "He's gone. The circus people came to take him away, and there was nothing I could do to stop them. I couldn't even try, so I just had to give him back."

She dissolved into huge, shuddering tears, and Maud and Enid cuddled up on either side of her like bookends.

"What were they like?" asked Enid. "Were they horrible? Do you think that's why he ran away?"

"He didn't run away," said Mildred between sobs. "He fell out of his crate while they were travelling—and he's not called Star; his real name is Binky. I saw the picture of him on the circus poster. He was sitting on a pony, and there was a seal, too. It was definitely him—he really *is* their dog. I just wish they weren't going to keep him in a crate, now that he's got used to being with me all the time. I'm going to miss him so much."

"Well," said Enid, "there's no use getting in a state about it if there's nothing to be done."

"I suppose that's true," said Maud, "and it's lunch break now and we've got double chanting afterwards, and Miss Bat's got a test ready, so you'll just have to get up and get on with it, Millie."

"I know you're right," said Mildred, climbing out of bed, wiping her eyes, and gently putting Tabby on the pillow, "and I *know* I can't, but I *so* wish I could do something to get him back."

CHAPTER ELEVEN

AFTER DOUBLE chanting, which had an extremely complicated rhythm that was virtually impossible to get right, Mildred sneaked into the playground with Tabby to reintroduce him to flying on a broomstick. Poor Tabby thought that Mildred was taking him for a little carry around the school, and nearly fainted with shock when she commanded the broomstick to hover and proceeded to put him on the back. As ever, he sat frozen in terror, then suddenly took a flying leap onto the wall. Mildred held out her arms to him, but he skittered along the top as fast as he could and jumped through a window, disappearing out of sight.

"*Oh* dear, Mildred," said a voice behind her. "Having cat trouble again?"

It was Ethel, with Drusilla beside her as usual. "So where's the circus dog?" she continued. "How come poor old Stripey's back on the broom — or *not,* as the case may be?"

"You *know* about this, don't you?" said Mildred, glaring at Ethel. "That's why you've come to gloat!"

Ethel was wearing her you'll-never-find-out expression, but Drusilla couldn't look Mildred in the eye and was actually blushing.

"*You* know about it too, don't you, Drusilla?" challenged Mildred, her voice rising with anger and tears. "Well, I hope you're both really pleased with yourselves."

"Poor old Mildred," sneered Ethel as Mildred grabbed her broomstick and marched out of the playground.

"Well, at least we'll see how good she really is at flying, now that she's back with her stupid cat," said Drusilla.

"Yes," agreed Ethel. "Anyway, she was cheating, having a circus dog as her broom companion. Everything's back to normal now: Mildred Hubble is the worst witch in the school, just as it should be."

CHAPTER TWELVE

THINGS HAD BEEN going so smoothly for Mildred, who had been really enjoying herself, confident at last that she could hold her head up among her classmates. Without Star she had taken an instant nosedive and found herself right back at square one.

"It was just like surfing," she explained to Maud and Enid when they were sitting in the broom shed, taking shelter during a rainy lunch break. "You know, zipping along on the top of a wave, having a brilliant time, taking everything for granted, and then—BANG!—you hit a rock, and everything just falls to pieces."

"Not *everything*," said Enid.

"Well, it *feels* like everything," said Mildred gloomily. "I can't tell you how nice it was to finally be good at flying—and the more praise I got from the teachers, the better I got at everything else. It encouraged me to try harder—but it wasn't really *me*, was it? It was Star who was brilliant at flying, and he sort of admired me—you know what dogs are like—so *I* had to keep up with *him*, not the other way round. Now that I'm back with Tabby, everyone can see I'm like a beginner, as Ethel never stops pointing out. She's right, really. I *am* a hopeless case—everything I do always *does* go wrong in the end."

"Well, it *sort* of does," said Maud, "but then it sort of doesn't, because usually, when it's gone disastrously wrong, something happens to save the day—like when you won the swimming-pool competition—"

"And rescuing Mr. Rowan Webb," said Enid.

"*And* finding the treasure on our school holiday after Miss Hardbroom was knocked out in the boat," said Maud. "That looked fairly hopeless at the time, didn't it? Do you know what I think, Millie?" she continued cheerfully. "I think you've got a magic pixie keeping an eye on you. Something will happen to get things back on an even keel for you. It always has done before, so I don't see why it won't this time."

"It's logical, my dear," said Enid kindly, doing a very good impersonation of Miss Cackle. "We just have to wait patiently and everything will turn out fine—meanwhile, let's all have a biscuit!"

Mildred couldn't help smiling at her friends, who were always on hand to cheer her up.

"I don't know what I'd do without you two," she said as they all huddled up and leaned against one another affectionately. "Although I honestly can't see how I can get myself out of this particular nosedive."

"I just *told* you," said Maud. "You don't have to do anything at all except wait and see."

CHAPTER THIRTEEN

MILDRED *did* try to heed Maud's advice and wait patiently for things to start looking up, but in reality they seemed to be going from bad to worse.

For a start, after several months off from flying, Tabby couldn't cope at all. Mildred spent most of her time hauling him out from under her bed or pursuing him down the corridors, which was most embarrassing, especially when Ethel was watching. Sadly, it didn't take long before Mildred found it impossible to concentrate on anything, and she was soon back at the bottom of the class in all subjects.

One night she had a horrible dream about Star. He often featured in her dreams (usually happy ones, although these made her sad when she woke up and found they weren't real), but this one was a nightmare. In the dream, Star was locked up in a crate with a thunderstorm raging outside, and she was flying around, dodging lightning bolts while trying to get him out.

Mildred woke with a jolt. She was partly glad that it had only been a dream, but she also had an unsettled feeling that the little dog might have been trying to send her a telepathic message. The dream had seemed so *real*.

It was just getting light. Outside the window a cloudless, windless day was beckoning. Someone had mentioned to Mildred that the circus was now pitched at Queen's Warren, a large market town fifteen miles on from Greater Bustling. She could easily get there and back in time for the rising bell—just to make sure that Star had settled into his old routine and was reasonably happy.

However, she hadn't thought about what she would actually *do* if he wasn't.

"Where on earth are you going, Mildred?" whispered Maud, who had opened her door to let her cat in and found Mildred creeping down the shadowy corridor. "You're not running away, are you?" she asked. "Just as well I got up early to revise for H.B.'s ultra-important potions test. You do realize it's our first lesson, don't you?"

Another door creaked open and Enid peered out, blinking at Maud and Mildred, who had stopped in her doorway.

"What's going on?" she asked in a just-woken-up, croaky voice.

"Mildred's obviously *up* to something," whispered Maud.

"Well, you'd better both come in here," whispered Enid, "or we'll wake the whole corridor."

Mildred and Maud stepped into Enid's room and closed the door.

"Look," said Mildred. "I can't stop. I'm just nipping to Queen's Warren to make sure Star's all right. I had a horrible dream about him and I want to check that he's OK. I'm not going to steal him or anything—and I'll be back before the rising bell."

"You're just *nipping* to Queen's Warren!" exclaimed Maud. "You've never even been there, Mildred! You'll get lost, and H.B. will go bonkers when she finds out."

Enid grabbed her cardigan and started putting it on over her pyjamas.

"Come on, Maud," she said as she pulled on her cloak. "We'll have to go with her. I've got a bat-nav so we won't get lost, *and* we'll get there much, much faster."

"What's a *bat-nav*?" asked Mildred and Maud, intrigued.

"It's a specially trained long-eared bat," explained Enid. "You say the name of a town or village into a special device clipped to its ear, which translates it into sonar squeaks, and the bat just takes you there like magic."

"Wow!" exclaimed Maud. "Are they actually allowed?"

"'Course they aren't," said Enid, "but *I* won't tell if *you* won't."

"Are you coming then, Maud?" asked Mildred.

Maud hesitated. She most definitely *didn't* want to set out on such a perilous journey, abandoning her early-morning revision. On the other hand, she didn't want to abandon her best friend either, especially now that Enid was definitely going with her.

"Hang on," said Maud. "I'll get my cloak and hat and meet you at the broom shed."

The bat-nav halved the journey time. Maud and Mildred were fascinated as the little brown bat danced along ahead of them, leading the way.

"Won't he want to go to sleep soon?" asked Mildred. "The sun's getting bright."

"Nope," said Enid. "They're specially trained to fly whenever you give them instructions, whatever hour of the day. Brilliant, isn't it? Look, there's the circus!"

The clock tower in the town square at Queen's Warren showed six o'clock as they glided past it to the outskirts of the town, where they could clearly see the red-and-white-striped big top, plus a large caravan, several cage-like metal crates and containers, and two flatbed trucks.

A small, fat pony with an overgrown mane and tail was tethered in the field next to the crates. He shook the hair from his eyes and looked up curiously as the three witches skimmed silently over him, landing out of sight behind the big top.

The girls parked their broomsticks with their hats perched on top, and Enid settled the bat-nav with a stick wedged under the brim of her hat so that he could hang upside down and have a rest.

Star was in one of the crates, and he began barking wildly when he saw Mildred creeping past.

"He's in here," gasped Mildred, thrilled to find him so easily. "Stop it, boy. Shh! It's all right; it's all right."

But it clearly wasn't all right. The crate was cramped and dark with its heavy canvas cover, and it was more than Mildred could bear, seeing him imprisoned, frenziedly barking and trying to lick her hands through the bars.

"I *knew* this wasn't a good idea," muttered Maud.

"OK," said Enid, trying to sound jaunty. "It's not the Ritz, but you knew he was going to be kept in a crate between shows. He's fine. Come on — let's go before he wakes everyone up."

But it was too late. The caravan door crashed open, and there was Mr. Brilliantine, wrapped in a maroon silk dressing gown.

"What are you up to?" he thundered. "Hilda!" he called behind him. "We seem to have visitors."

CHAPTER FOURTEEN

EVER THE peacemaker, Maud rushed forward.

"We're so sorry to have woken you," she said politely. "We've come from Miss Cackle's Academy. It's just that Mildred's been so unhappy without Star—I mean, Binky—that she wanted a quick cuddle before school! We really didn't mean to wake you, so we'll be off now. Come on, Mildred!" she said, grabbing Mildred by the arm.

Enid grabbed her other arm, and they yanked her away from the crate. Mrs. Brilliantine had now come out onto the

caravan doorstep, wearing a green satin dressing gown with an orange feather collar, covered in bright pink embroidered flamingos.

"I recognize you," she said, peering at Mildred. "You're the girl who looked after our Binky when he was lost. How did you *get* here?" she asked, suddenly noticing their assortment of cloaks and pyjamas.

"Well—um—er..." said Mildred. "We—"

"Got a lift," announced Enid.

"From my aunt!" added Maud. "She was just passing, so she said she'd drop us here."

"At six o'clock in the morning?" queried Mr. Brilliantine. "Where on earth was she going at such a time?"

"To . . . um . . . er . . . the hairdresser's!" announced Mildred desperately.

"She works from home—the hairdresser, that is," continued Enid, noting the astonished look on Mr. and Mrs. Brilliantine's faces.

"She starts at the crack of dawn," explained Mildred, "so she can fit everyone in. She's very popular. People have to make appointments months ahead."

"Well, your aunt obviously isn't back yet," said Mrs. Brilliantine.

"That's because she's getting her hair coloured," Mildred announced wildly. "It takes hours, so she'll be ages yet."

"Well, you'd better join us for breakfast then," said Mrs. Brilliantine in a kindly voice.

"She's got very long hair!" Mildred burbled on, beginning to believe that Maud really did have a long-haired aunt who was taking ages at a real hairdresser's.

"I'm sure she does," said Mr. Brilliantine distractedly. "Hilda, could you let Binky out of his crate before he does himself an injury? I'll go and put the kettle on."

The three witches couldn't believe their luck when Mr. Brilliantine went off to make them tea and toast, while Mrs. Brilliantine unlocked Binky/Star's crate. He hurtled out, straight into Mildred's arms, knocking her over onto the grass. Maud and Enid joined in, rolling about and patting him while he tried to wash all three of them at once.

CHAPTER FIFTEEN

WHILE THEY were waiting for their breakfast, Mrs. Brilliantine took them to look round the big top. It was small and old-fashioned, exactly like a circus you might see in a picture book, with a trapeze hanging from the centre, and three rows of benches surrounding a ring with a sawdust floor.

"Would you like to meet Spotty, our seal?" asked Mrs. Brilliantine, who was being so friendly that the girls were beginning to enjoy themselves.

The seal was in a large crate with a tiny

pool at one end. She was sitting in the murky water looking sad, and the girls were upset to see her in such an unappealing space.

"She doesn't look very happy," ventured Mildred, trying not to sound disapproving in case Mrs. Brilliantine stopped being nice to them.

"She's *never* very happy," said Mrs. Brilliantine. "I don't know why we keep her, really. We found her on a beach and have tried everything to train her, but she's useless—can't even balance a ball on her nose."

"The pony's not much better," complained Mr. Brilliantine as he came to find them, bringing an inviting breakfast tray and setting it down on an upturned packing case. "He trots around the ring, and that's *it* as far as he's concerned! It's our Binky who is the star of the show with all his jumping and twirling, and of course the kids love him because he's so cute."

"They like your clown act too," said Mrs. Brilliantine encouragingly.

"And you too, my dear," said Mr. Brilliantine fondly. "So graceful on the flying trapeze."

Gloom settled on the three friends as they sat around the packing case munching their toast. Time was getting on, and any minute now Star would have to go back into his crate with a broken heart, and Mildred would have to brace herself to say good-bye all over again.

Miss Hardbroom had been right. Mildred had only made things worse for both of them. And now that she knew about Spotty the sad seal, Mildred would worry about her too. She found herself wishing that she had never come.

"Well, girls," said Mrs. Brilliantine as they made their way back to the caravan, "will you be all right waiting for your aunt out here while we get ourselves ready for the day?"

She picked up Star in a firm hold and carried him, yelping, back to his crate.

"Thank you for our breakfast," said Mildred, managing not to cry. "It was very kind of you to let me see him again."

"That's all right," said Mrs. Brilliantine. "I can tell that you and Binky have a real bond. To be honest, you could take all three animals home with you if there was something to replace them, but there isn't, so our little star attraction will have to stay."

As soon as the caravan door closed, Enid and Maud grabbed Mildred and frog-marched her round the back of the big top to their broomsticks and hats. The bat-nav was so deeply asleep that he had to be prodded awake before Enid could reprogram him.

"Are you feeling all right, Mildred?" asked Maud, noting her miserable expression as they rose vertically and sped away.

"Not really," said Mildred. "I just *hate* to see unhappy animals, that's all. It's such a waste of Star, leaving him in a crate all day, and Spotty wasn't having a great time either—even the pony looked fed up."

Mildred glanced back wistfully at the striped tent, which was already a tiny speck behind them. "I so wish there was something we could do," she said.

"Well, there isn't," said Maud firmly. "And right now we'd better follow that bat and get home before the rising bell."

CHAPTER SIXTEEN

"IF ONLY I could *ask* the animals if they were all right," said Mildred fretfully to Maud a few days later when they were sitting in the playground. "I mean, it looks awful to *us*, the way they live, but *they* might not mind as much as we would."

"Actually," said Maud, "you *could* ask them, if you use that speaking spell you invented last year. Then they could tell you what it's really like, being in the circus day in, day out."

"What a brilliant idea, Maudie!" said Mildred. "I'll borrow Enid's bat-nav and sneak back tomorrow morning before the circus moves on. I know where Star's crate is now, so I'll tell him to be quiet as soon as I arrive. He's really good at keeping quiet after hiding in my room when I found him. And even if he does wake the Brilliantines up, I'll just say I'm visiting again — they didn't seem to mind last time!"

Maud was only too happy that Mildred wanted to go on her own, as she was still hoping for the First Prize in Team Spirit and did not want to spoil her chances.

"Well, if you're sure," she said. "Just be careful to leave early — Enid and I will think up an excuse if you're late coming back."

"Thank goodness it's summer," thought Mildred as she hovered over the school gates the next morning. The sun was just rising into another perfect day, and Mildred could see for miles ahead. She had borrowed Enid's bat-nav, which was flittering along in front of her.

When she was up early on her broom, Mildred often noticed unusual wildlife, and on this particular morning she suddenly found herself in the middle of a cloud of skylarks. She watched entranced as they

twirled up and down like tiny helicopters, singing their exquisite "good morning" to the world. No need for a speaking spell to understand what these exuberant little birds were telling her: "Hello, world! Such a beautiful day! So nice to be up and about before anyone else!"

She touched down beside the big top in record time. It was only five thirty, and the blinds were still tightly drawn in the caravan. She parked her broomstick and the bat-nav, and crept silently through the damp grass to the front of Star's crate. Mercifully, he was fast asleep, so she sat and watched him fondly for a minute or two.

"Star," she whispered. "Wake up, and no barking."

He had been dreaming that he was curled up under Mildred's bed with Tabby, so he was overjoyed to find that she was really

there. He managed to restrain himself from barking, and Mildred unbolted the crate and let him out for a silent cuddle that went on for ages. At last she put him down, with a finger to her lips, then she untethered the pony and led him round to the seal's crate.

Mildred had brought a tape measure with her so that she could measure the animals to work out the precise formula for the speaking spell. The measurements had to be perfect or the spell wouldn't work.

"Right then, Star," she said. "You first."

CHAPTER SEVENTEEN

DID I get it right?" asked Mildred. "Can you speak?"

"You did!" woofed Star. "I can."

"Quietly," she whispered. "Not a word — don't say anything just for one moment while I magic the others."

The pony was very good about being measured, as he often had a saddle and reins put on and was used to standing still, but the seal was more tricky. She wasn't keen at all and flumped off into the pool the minute the door was unbolted. Mildred had to crawl in to get the tape measure around her. The crate was slimy and smelled of old fish, so it was not very nice for Mildred, inching her way along on her hands and knees to the pool, where the nervous seal was pressed against the bars. Then she had to wriggle out backward, feeling slightly sick, so that she could work out the sizes for each animal's spell.

Both spells worked, and all three animals began talking excitedly at once — Mildred could barely hear what they were saying!

"Shh!" she commanded in a loud whisper. "One at a time, please, and keep your voices down. Spotty," she said, pointing at the seal, "you first."

The seal shuffled forward importantly.

"My name isn't Spotty," she said in a soft, gentle voice, almost as if she was singing. "It's really Selkie, after the creature in the myth—you know, the one that's half seal, half human—and I'm not a performing seal at all. I was lost on the beach, and the Brilliantines found me at a place called Grim Cove. There's a colony of us there, and I so want to go back and join my family. Common seals don't *do* tricks— well, we can do one: it's pretending to be a banana. Look, I'll do it now if you like— all common seals can do it naturally," she said proudly.

Mildred had to stop herself laughing as Selkie curved her body and flippers into a perfect banana shape.

"That's truly wonderful," said Mildred

with a smile. "And I *know* Grim Cove—a friend of mine owns a castle there."

"You *know* where it is?" gasped Selkie. "Can you take me back there? I hate it here. I'm just no good at *anything*, and I can never seem to please them, whatever I do."

"I know how you feel about *that*," agreed Mildred earnestly. Next, she turned to the pony. "What about you?" she asked. "Do you like being here?"

"Not much," he replied in a voice with a whinny, as if he was clearing his throat. "It's not *that* bad. I mean, I get food and lots of rest, and I don't mind trotting around the ring with Binky on my back—"

101

"I'm not Binky," muttered Star crossly. "My real name is Star. Mildred gave it to me, and I belong to her, not the Brilliantines." He gave Mildred an adoring look that melted her heart.

"Sorry, Bink—I mean Star—" continued the pony. "*I've* got the wrong name too. I was renamed Mr. Smartie, but my real name is Merlin, and I used to belong to a darling little girl. Then her parents had to sell me so she could go to boarding school, and the Brilliantines bought me. She was a really nice little girl and she took such care of me—I'd give anything to see her again. Do you think you could help me get out of here? I get so lonely standing in a field all day."

"And we *all* hate the travelling," continued Selkie. "It's really horrible being stuck in a crate, jolting along on the back of a truck."

Mildred turned to Star. "How about you?" she asked. "How do *you* feel about living here?"

"To be truthful," he said, "I came here as a puppy, so I didn't mind it too much because I didn't know any other way of life. I quite enjoyed doing my acrobatic acts each evening, though it did get a bit boring being left outside and sleeping so much. Then I fell out of the crate when we were on the move, and you found me, and that was wonderful. But when the Brilliantines took me back, I hated every minute here because I knew what I was missing — it was you! Can I come home with you? *Please?*"

"Can I come too?" asked Merlin. "I'd work for you. I wouldn't be any trouble!"

"Me too," said Selkie. "Don't leave me here. If you could just get me back to Grim Cove, I could sit on the rocks with my family and go diving into the deep cold water—mmmm!"

"*PLEEEEEEASE!*" they all pleaded at once.

Mildred gazed at the three earnest creatures, staring at her with eyes full of hope and trust, and wondered what on earth she was going to do now.

"You won't just leave us here, will you?" asked Star. "You won't just fly off and never come back?"

"Of course I won't," said Mildred firmly, trying to sound like a person in charge. "I *will* have to go back to school for a week or so while I think up a plan, but I'll definitely be back to collect all of you."

The three pairs of eyes stared into her very soul.

"I promise on my honour," she continued. "Meanwhile, don't say a human word in front of the Brilliantines. Speaking animals in a circus — just imagine it. They'd *never* let you go! So you must take great care. Quickly now, back into your crates and the field, and I'll get you locked in and tethered. Not for much longer, though — I'll be back. All you have to do is trust me and wait — and no talking!"

CHAPTER EIGHTEEN

NOW CAME THE difficult part. Mildred had promised on her honour that she would rescue all three circus animals — but she hadn't the faintest idea how she could possibly achieve that.

"Whatever made you promise to rescue *all* of them?" asked Maud crossly while she and Enid were helping Mildred with an extra flying lesson for Tabby. "You won't even be able to rescue *Star* unless the Brilliantines agree. You can't just go charging in there and steal them." At this point Maud tried (and failed) to grab Tabby, who had suddenly leapt straight up and over the wall, as agile as a squirrel.

Mildred sat down on her hovering broom.

"I don't know why you're sounding so cross," she muttered. "*You're* not the one who promised. *I'm* the one who has to think up a plan and put it into practice!"

"That's not strictly true," said Enid. "If you come up with a workable plan, you're going to need some help transporting three large animals, especially the seal. *I'm* not too worried about getting into trouble, as I'm not trying for an award, but Maudie's set her heart on First Prize for Team Spirit."

"Well, it *would* be team spirit, helping your friends," said Mildred.

"It wouldn't be the right *sort* of team spirit, though," said Maud. "Leaving school premises without permission, probably using unauthorized spells—we'd all be lucky not to get expelled, let alone win a first prize for anything."

"Anyway," said Enid as Tabby reappeared on top of the wall several metres away, yowling miserably, "you've got to come up with a good plan first."

"The annoying thing is," said Mildred, "the Brilliantines *said* that they'd give us all three animals if someone could come up with a crowd-pulling replacement act. They actually said it to us—don't you remember?" She held her arms out to Tabby, who looked the other way and didn't budge.

"So, we have to think up two plans," said Enid brightly. "Plan one: we have to find a great replacement act to offer the Brilliantines. And plan two: what to do with Selkie and Merlin if the Brilliantines let us have them all."

Mildred had been inching her way along the playground wall and suddenly made a grab for Tabby, who leapt into the air, landed neatly a metre away, and disappeared through a convenient window.

"That will be two virtually impossible plans then," said Maud flatly. "We'll never manage it."

"Don't say that," said Mildred. "I promised, on my honour, to rescue all three of them, so I have to come up with something. There must be a solution — there *has* to be."

CHAPTER NINETEEN

MILDRED was shaken awake the very next morning by an excited Enid. It was hours before the rising bell, and Mildred had been deeply asleep, dreaming that she was trying to hold on to a slippery and upset Selkie, who was sliding off her broomstick.

"Gosh, Enid," said Mildred, moving Tabby, who had been draped on top of her, and propping herself up on one elbow. "I was having such an awful dream—thanks for waking me. Why *did* you wake me? It's really early . . ."

"I've cracked it!" exclaimed Enid. "Well, I've cracked the first part of the plan, so it's a start. I've thought up an act that we can offer the Brilliantines in exchange for the animals."

"Oh, wow!" said Mildred. "Go on, tell me!"

"Easy-peasy," said Enid. "Don't know why we didn't think of it straightaway. It's our Privilege Spell—you know, the one where we can enchant any sort of brush. We could do a flying dustpan and brush for Mr. Brilliantine when he's being a clown, and a big yard broom for them to do acrobatics on. *And* a whole load of toothbrushes in different colours—they'd be really cute even without the snails, and they could fly through the audience. Do you remember that Miss Drill said you had to deactivate the brushes or anyone could use them? Well, we just won't take the spell off. Then the Brilliantines could use them forever."

"Wow, Enid!" said Mildred, impressed. "That's such a brilliant idea!"

Enid smiled. "It is, isn't it? A brilliant idea for the Brilliantines! Let's go and tell Maud."

"Hmmm," said Mildred. "She's not going to be too happy about this."

"Shall we just not tell her?" asked Enid. "Then she won't feel that she has to come, so she'll be safe if anything goes wrong? I really would hate it if she lost out on First Prize for Team Spirit."

"Tricky," said Mildred. "She might be hurt if we sneaked off without her. I think it's best if we *tell* her but insist that she doesn't come."

The brush-exchange idea was actually an excellent plan, and soon Maud was up to her neck in it with the other two. Although it was a bit risky, she knew it might just work, and she couldn't bear to be left out.

"You don't *have* to come, Maudie," said Mildred, stuffing twenty-five brightly coloured toothbrushes into her satchel. "Just in case there are a few awkward things to explain later."

"Like these toothbrushes!" exclaimed Maud. "Where did you get them?"

"From the bathroom supplies cupboard," said Mildred. "There are stacks of them behind the toilet rolls. No one's going to check, and we can replace them later."

"And I've got one of the yard brooms

under my bed," said Enid. "It's the spare one from the Big Playground. They'll never notice. I've got that nice green dustpan and brush from the cloakroom too. It's always stuffed at the back of the boot locker, so it won't be missed."

"Well, I suppose we'd better set off soon and get on with it," said Maud.

"The sooner, the better," agreed Mildred. "We've been dithering about for nearly two weeks since I last saw them, and they'll be wondering if we're ever going to come and rescue them. Let's go at first light tomorrow," she said to Enid. "We can come to your room and help you with the yard broom and the dustpan."

"OK," said Enid. "I'll program the bat-nav."

"Right," said Maud reluctantly.

"That settles it then," said Mildred. "Tomorrow morning it is!"

CHAPTER TWENTY

THEY DIDN'T really need the bat-nav. Now that Mildred had flown to Queen's Warren twice, it was easy to recognize landmark villages and towns on the way. On the other hand, it was nice just to follow the bat so that they could chat with one another without having to concentrate on the route.

The weather was perfect again, with only a light breeze, which made balancing easy. Enid had already enchanted the yard broom because it was too cumbersome to carry, and had tethered it to her broomstick to keep it going in the right direction.

Maud had stuffed the dustpan and brush into her backpack, ready to be enchanted when they arrived, along with the toothbrushes crammed into Mildred's satchel.

"If they *do* agree to our swap," said Maud, "what are we actually going to do with the seal and the pony?"

"Not absolutely sure about that," mumbled Mildred.

"One thing we *must* do," said Enid, "if they actually agree to the swap, is get a

116

letter from the Brilliantines to show Miss Cackle. Otherwise it will look as if we've stolen all their animals."

"Good thinking, Eenie-meeny," said Maud, "but what *are* we doing to do with them all?"

"I'm sure Miss Cackle would let me have Star back anyway," said Mildred, "and perhaps they could keep the pony for riding lessons! Pentangle's has two ponies — it might attract more pupils to our school. Miss Cackle would love that."

"And the seal?" asked Maud.

"Let's cross that bridge when we come to it," said Mildred. "Look, we've arrived!"

They parked their broomsticks and the bat-nav in the usual place and set about enchanting the dustpan and brush, which immediately began capering about, the brush chasing the pan. Maud grabbed the brush in one hand and the dustpan in the other and hung on tightly.

Mildred shook the toothbrushes out of her satchel onto the grass.

"Could you enchant all these individually?" she asked Enid. "You'll have to trap them back in the satchel, ready to show the Brilliantines, or they might go bobbing off and get lost. I'll go and wake everyone up."

Waking everyone up had already happened. Star was barking his head off, Selkie was honking, and Merlin was whinnying and neighing. Mildred counted the days on her fingers and realized that exactly two weeks had passed, so the spell had worn off and they could no longer speak. She knelt down to scratch Star's head through the bars, and he blinked his eyes and gazed at her.

"We don't have to speak to each other anyway," she said tenderly. "Just a look will do."

"Arrff," woofed Star. *"Woof, WOOF!"*

The caravan door crashed open, and Mr. and Mrs. Brilliantine emerged in their dressing gowns, looking half-asleep and annoyed.

"Not you again!" said Mr. Brilliantine. "Why do you always have to come at such an unearthly hour?"

"Actually," said Mildred, "we've brought some things with us, to give you in exchange for the animals. That's if you think they're a good idea, of course. They're sort of magical props for a showstopping act to bring in huge audiences. You'll probably have to buy a bigger big top!"

Mr. and Mrs. Brilliantine exchanged unimpressed glances.

"It's a really *good* idea," said Mildred enthusiastically. "I just know you're going to love it."

"All right, then," said Mr. Brilliantine. "You might as well show us what you've brought, now that you're here."

CHAPTER TWENTY-ONE

EVERYTHING WENT like clock-work in the big top. The Brilliantines were simply aston-ished by the display put on by Mildred and her two best friends.

Mildred and Enid sat on the bristle end of the yard broom and flew it up to the trapeze, then took it sedately around the top of the tent. Maud allowed herself to be chased by the dustpan and brush, both of which got slightly out of hand and had to be stuffed

into Maud's backpack. But it was the twenty-five pretty toothbrushes that clinched the deal. They were utterly charming, swooping

and diving in an orderly line wherever Mildred sent them, and flying back politely into her satchel as soon as she asked them to.

"How does it all work?" asked Mr.

Brilliantine, picking up a toothbrush, which lay motionless in his hand. "How do you switch them on? Do they run on batteries? How long will they last?"

"They'll last forever," said Mildred, "with no maintenance — you just have to speak to them in a particular way. I'll show you how in a moment. And you have to be very firm with the dustpan and brush. The yard broom is fine, and the toothbrushes are a dream, but for some reason the dustpan and brush have a bit of a wild streak, so you have to show them who's boss! Shall we give you some lessons?"

The Brilliantines spent the next hour flying up to the trapeze on the yard broom, launching the toothbrushes around the empty benches, and being chased by the extremely naughty dustpan and brush. Mr. Brilliantine could see how much fun this would be during his clown performance, and Mrs. Brilliantine could certainly see how much more fun it would be to fly up to the trapeze before she did her routine. Within minutes they were completely hooked on their new magic equipment.

"We could leave you the backpack like a sort of kennel for the dustpan and brush," said Maud helpfully.

"And you can have my satchel for the toothbrushes," said Mildred. "They settle down really quickly in there."

"The yard broom's fine anywhere," said Enid. "It's very laid-back and no trouble at all."

"*Will* you swap with us, then?" said Mildred. "Our magic brushes in exchange for the seal, the pony, and the dog?"

Mr. and Mrs. Brilliantine twinkled at each other.

"Done!" they said in unison, laughing.

CHAPTER TWENTY-TWO

AS SOON AS the Brilliantines had written their letter of new owner-ship for Mildred to present to Miss Cackle, they disappeared inside the caravan to change into their costumes so that they could start practicing their routine, and the girls rushed over to the animals to tell them the good news.

"So," said Maud, "what *are* we going to do with the seal?"

"It's OK," said Mildred. "I thought this out in bed last night. I already know where she wants to go — back to her colony at Grim Cove — so all we have to do is a transference spell and—*hey, presto!*—she'll be back with her family, telling them all about what happened. Won't you, Selkie? Is that where you'd like to go? If you can understand me, do a banana for me."

Immediately Selkie curved herself into the banana shape, waving one flipper and honking happily.

"That's sorted, then," Mildred responded, laughing. "And I've written out the transference spell, so we can do it right now."

Mildred smoothed Selkie's damp head.

"I must admit, being transferred does feel a bit weird," she told her. "H.B. did it to me once and you feel sort of squashed and pulled at the same time, but don't worry, because it's all over in a few seconds, and then you suddenly arrive where you've been sent. Just think of splashing down in Grim Cove, and don't forget to keep your eyes shut as there are lots of bright lights and stars."

"Gosh, Millie," said Enid admiringly. "You've really planned this perfectly."

"Can you get a move on?" asked Maud nervously. "We can't possibly get back before the rising bell, and they're bound to see us flying in."

"But we've got our ownership letter to show Miss Cackle," said Mildred. "And Selkie will be safely back in the sea by the time we get home, so there's nothing to worry about."

"Relax, Maud," said Enid. "Nothing can go wrong now."

CHAPTER TWENTY-THREE

THERE WAS still half an hour before morning assembly, and Miss Cackle was sitting in the staff room with Miss Hardbroom, beginning their assessment of all the Year Four pupils in order to pick the worthiest recipients for the various prizes at the end of Summer Term.

"I was wondering if we could have a First Prize for Art this year?" suggested Miss Cackle.

"I thought we'd decided this already," replied Miss Hardbroom wearily. "We were both in *complete* agreement that prizes would be awarded for serious subjects relating to the ethos of the school."

"Yes, I do know that," said Miss Cackle. "It's just that, well, Mildred Hubble is so very talented at art, and it seems a shame that there is no award for it."

"I'm sorry, Miss Cackle, but I really think that a prize for art would be the thin end of the wedge in a fine academic school like this," continued Miss Hardbroom, somehow managing to make the word *art* sound unsavoury. "I seem to remember that you have already sneaked in a prize for the tidiest room, as a sop to less academic pupils — which, incidentally, most certainly won't be won by Mildred Hubble! Have you seen her room lately?"

At this point, to their great astonishment, the door suddenly crashed open and an irate Miss Bat barged into the room, wearing her swimming costume with a towel wrapped round her shoulders.

"Really!" she exclaimed. "As if frogs and

water snails aren't bad enough, but to swim straight into a *seal* when one is taking an early-morning dip is the last straw — one just doesn't *expect* it!"

"Did you say a *seal*, Miss Bat?" asked Miss Cackle in disbelieving tones.

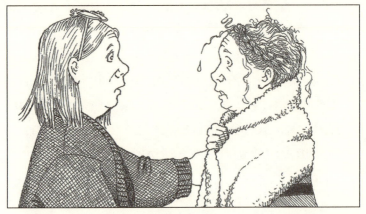

"I most certainly did," quavered Miss Bat. "I know what a seal looks like! It appeared out of nowhere and splashed down in the deep end. Then it plunged under the water and surfaced right in front of me, making a sort of honking sound — that is the only way to describe it! Well, I got out smartish, I can tell you!"

"There, there, Miss Bat," soothed Miss Cackle, placing an arm round Miss Bat's towel-clad shoulders and leading her to the door. "Why don't you go and get into some nice dry clothes and come back here for some lovely tea and biscuits? I'll speak to Miss Drill, and she can sort it out as soon as possible."

She gently nudged Miss Bat out of the staff room and closed the door.

"I really do think it might be time for Miss Bat to retire," she continued sadly, suddenly noticing that Miss Hardbroom was staring out of the window.

"Come and take a look at this, Miss Cackle," said Miss Hardbroom, her voice harsh with annoyance. "It's Mildred Hubble and Co. down there by the gate — and it looks as if she's decided to rescue her magical mutt from the circus. It also looks as if she's stolen a pony at the same time — and she's got Enid Nightshade and Maud Spellbody assisting her in this folly. I really thought Maud would have had more sense."

"Oh *dear*," said Miss Cackle. "Such a very silly thing to do. They *must* realize that they'll have to take them straight back again."

"They certainly will," said Miss Hardbroom briskly. "We'd better go down and nip this in the bud before it goes any further."

The journey back to school had taken longer than expected, with Merlin trotting along beneath them and Star on his back. The three young witches had been flying overhead as low as possible, taking care

not to crash into the treetops, calling out Merlin's name to keep him going in the right direction. They also had to slow down and wait every now and then, so that he could have a rest. Merlin was exhausted when they finally arrived at the school gates, but Star couldn't contain his joy and started barking and twirling.

"Shh," said Mildred, glancing around nervously. "We've got some explaining to do before H.B. finds out about this."

"You most certainly have," agreed Miss Hardbroom, materializing right next to the petrified pony, who could sense that she was not friendly. "Perhaps you could start by telling me precisely what you think you are doing—*all* of you."

The three friends stood frozen with fear as it suddenly dawned on them that this might not be as simple as they had thought. Pupils at Miss Cackle's were never encouraged to take matters into their own hands, and their behaviour would be met with disapproval, however worthy their motives.

Miss Cackle came out into the playground and bustled across to the gates. Unlike Miss Hardbroom, she preferred to use normal methods of arrival, such as walking up stairs and opening doors, only using magic on very special occasions.

Maud and Enid both had their arms around Merlin's neck, and Mildred was clutching Star. All three of them looked exceptionally guilty.

"Perhaps *you'd* better explain, Mildred," coaxed Miss Cackle. "Surely you must know that you can't just take back something that isn't yours — and where did this pony come from?"

Mildred couldn't think how to begin. She opened her mouth to start and then closed it again.

"Well," said Miss Cackle, "it looks as if you've had a very long journey, so I think you'd better all come up to my study and have a cup of tea while we get to the bottom of this. What shall we do with the pony, Miss Hardbroom?" she continued, stroking Merlin's soft nose.

"Just leave him here," said Miss Hardbroom harshly. "He'll be going back where he came from in a very short while."

"But he'll need a rest after coming all that way," said Miss Cackle. "And a drink. We can find a first-year to fetch a bucket of water. Come along now, girls — I'm sure we can sort this out in no time."

On their way to Miss Cackle's study, they passed Dulcie.

136

"Ah, Dulcie," said Miss Cackle. "Just the person to run a little errand for me."

"Of course, Miss Cackle," said Dulcie politely.

"There's a pony in the playground, tethered to the gate," explained Miss Cackle. "Could you take him a bucket of water? He's had rather a long journey, and I seem to remember that you are especially fond of horses."

CHAPTER TWENTY-FOUR

EVERYONE HAD just sat down in Miss Cackle's study with a cup of tea when there was a loud knocking at the door.

"What *now*?" snapped Miss Hardbroom.

"Well, it sounds quite urgent," said Miss Cackle, "so I think we'd better find out. Come in!"

The heavy door creaked open and Dulcie tumbled into the room, her eyes shining.

"What is it, Dulcie?" asked Miss Cackle. "Is everything all right?"

"Oh, it's so much *more* than all right, Miss Cackle!" exclaimed Dulcie. "That pony, the one tied to the gate, it's Merlin! He was my pony before my parents sold him! If he's going to be here as our school pony, can I be the one to look after him? Please, Miss Cackle—I would look after him so well. He was just thrilled to see me again. Oh, Miss Cackle, I just can't believe that he's come to live at the school!"

"Calm down now," said Miss Cackle, looking fondly at the delighted first-year. "Nothing is settled yet, but if we *do* keep the pony, then you will certainly be at the top of my list of helpers. Off you go now—mustn't be late for lessons.

"Now then, Mildred," she continued as the door closed behind her, "may we have an explanation about the recent additions to your ever-growing menagerie?"

Mildred took out the letter signed by the Brilliantines and handed it to the headmistress.

"I think it would be simplest if you just read this, Miss Cackle," she said. "It's a document transferring ownership to me, signed by the Brilliantines, so it's perfectly legal. They've given us Star and Merlin—we thought you might like to keep a pony here for riding lessons. There was a seal, too, but we couldn't think what to do with her, so we transferred her back to the sea at Grim Cove—I saw a colony of common seals there once," she added, not wanting to admit that she had cast a speaking spell to find out where the seal had come from.

Miss Cackle and Miss Hardbroom exchanged knowing glances.

"When you cast the spell, Mildred," said

140

Miss Hardbroom, "did you make sure that you pictured Grim Cove in your mind, clearing your thoughts of *everything* else?"

"I *think* so," said Mildred, feeling a little unnerved.

"Are you sure that the school swimming pool wasn't in your thoughts at all?" asked Miss Cackle. "You do realize that your mind must be totally focused on the place of transfer when casting a transference spell? I was just wondering if you hadn't read the small paragraph at the end when you were looking up the spell."

Mildred began to feel uneasy. "Um," she murmured, suddenly remembering that she *had* been feeling a bit sad about saying good-bye to Selkie and had wondered for a mad moment if they could keep her in the swimming pool.

"Well, I did, sort of, *slightly* think of the swimming pool," she admitted, "but only round the *edges* of my mind. I was very much concentrating on Grim Cove in the *middle* of my mind—and much more than anything else!"

"That explains it," said Miss Hardbroom. "I have to tell you, Mildred, that there is, at this precise moment, a seal in the school swimming pool. Don't you find that a rather odd coincidence? It frightened Miss Bat out of her wits this morning, and we'll have to re-transfer it immediately before anything else untoward happens. Indeed, I rather think we should transfer it right now."

"Yes, yes," agreed Miss Cackle. "Miss Hardbroom, could you take the girls with you? I think we should make absolutely sure that it *is* the seal from the circus."

Miss Hardbroom led the way through the maze of corridors to the swimming pool, with the girls trooping along behind, suddenly feeling exhausted after their busy morning.

The pool seemed to be empty, the water dark and still.

"Shall I call her, Miss Hardbroom?" asked Mildred. "I could sit on the side and see if I can get her to come out. She's probably feeling a bit confused and scared."

Miss Hardbroom nodded, and Mildred crouched down by the water's edge.

"Selkie," she called softly. "It's me,

Mildred. I got the spell wrong—please come out. It's going to be all right now."

The bulrushes quivered, then stopped, and a few moments later, with bubbles and snorting, Selkie surfaced directly in front of Mildred.

"It's definitely our seal, Miss Hardbroom," she said. "Please could I just explain to her what happened?"

"Why on earth would you want to do that, Mildred?" asked Miss Hardbroom tetchily. "It's a seal—it won't know what you're talking about. Move aside now and let me do a *proper* transference spell. I really *don't* have all day to sort this out."

144

Mildred leaned forward and put her hand on Selkie's head.

"I know you can understand," she whispered. "H. B. might *seem* a bit cross, but she knows how to get you back to Grim Cove at once — she's the very best at spells! Shut your eyes and think of home."

Then Mildred looked up and said, "OK, Miss Hardbroom. You can do the transference spell now. She's ready."

"Take your hand off her head, Mildred," said Miss Hardbroom, "unless you want to go with her!"

"Sorry, Miss Hardbroom," said Mildred, hastily removing her hand. "Can you make sure she gets to Grim Cove this time? That's definitely where she wants to go."

"Grim Cove it is," said Miss Hardbroom.

After Selkie had been safely sent on her way, Miss Cackle summoned Miss Bat to

her study, and the girls apologized profusely about the failed transference spell and for ruining her morning swim.

"Not to worry, my dears," said Miss Bat cheerfully. "I'm just *so* glad that I wasn't imagining things."

"May I take Star with me?" asked Mildred, as Miss Cackle sent them to hang up their cloaks and hats, and to ask the kitchen staff for some late breakfast.

"You might as well," said Miss Cackle. "I'll talk to all three of you later when we've decided on our long-term plans for both the animals."

With relief, the three friends hurried out of the headmistress's study.

"I hope I haven't messed up my chances of First Prize for Team Spirit," said Maud anxiously.

"I can't see why," said Enid. "All three of us have displayed *brilliant* team spirit, if you ask me."

"What do you think they'll decide?" asked Maud. "I mean about Merlin and Star."

"No idea," said Mildred. "We'll just have to wait and see."

CHAPTER TWENTY-FIVE

I N MISS CACKLE'S STUDY, Miss Hardbroom was pondering the same question.

"What do you think we should do, Headmistress?" she asked, reading through the Brilliantines' document for the third time. "Do you think this note is genuine?"

"Yes, I do," said Miss Cackle. "Mildred Hubble is an honest pupil, and so is Maud. Enid might have been a little scatterbrained and attention-seeking when she first came here, but she's a different girl these days."

"But how did Mildred get them to change their minds?" Miss Hardbroom persisted.

"*And* to give up a pony *and* their performing seal? Mildred must have made some sort of bargain with them — it doesn't make sense otherwise. Shouldn't we press all three of them for more information?"

Miss Cackle smiled. "I don't think that will be necessary, Miss Hardbroom," she replied. "You and I both agree that this letter of ownership *is* genuine, so it would seem most logical to retire Mildred's poor unfortunate cat *again*, let Mildred have fun with Star, and advertise riding lessons in our coming year's prospectus — and it's *such* a pleasant coincidence that Merlin was Dulcie's pony in the first place. So there you are — everyone's happy and no harm done. No need to ask any awkward questions, wouldn't you agree, Miss Hardbroom?"

"Whatever you say, Miss Cackle," muttered Miss Hardbroom reluctantly. "You are the headmistress."

Mildred, Maud, and Enid were overjoyed when Miss Cackle sent for them the very next day and informed them that they could keep both Star and Merlin at the academy.

"You see, Maudie," said Mildred, smiling, "I *told* you it would all be fine."

"As long as they don't find out about the magic-brush exchange," said Maud.

"Oh, stop being such a worrywart," said Enid. "They won't find out—how could they?"

CHAPTER TWENTY-SIX

ETHEL and Drusilla were resting on their broomsticks, getting their breath back after a nosediving session in the playground. Through the gates, they could see Dulcie leading Merlin with a delighted friend on his back and several other pupils queuing for a ride.

"I don't know how she does it every time," grumbled Ethel.

"Dulcie?" asked Drusilla. "Well, she must be quite good with ponies, as Merlin used to belong to her."

"Not *Dulcie*," snarled Ethel scornfully. "I mean Mildred Hubble. How on earth did she get those circus people to give up all their animals — for nothing, as far as I can make out? If she didn't have the letter to prove it, I'd think she'd just stolen them. She *must* have given them something or they would never have let them go — especially the dog. He's excellent at acrobatics, even if he does look absolutely ridiculous on the back of a witch's broom."

"Miss Cackle didn't seem to think so," mused Drusilla, straying into dangerous waters. "Neither did the judges of the swimming-pool competition. Everyone agreed that Mildred could keep him as her broom companion in the end — even Miss Hardbroom."

Ethel narrowed her eyes and glared at Drusilla.

"Do you know, Drusilla," she said unpleasantly, "I really wonder why I'm friends with you sometimes. We don't think alike on anything and—"

"Oh, but we do," said Drusilla hastily. "Perhaps the letter *was* a forgery and Mildred just stole the animals. *I* know! Why don't we fly out to the circus tomorrow evening and do some detective work before it moves on somewhere else?"

"That's a really good idea, Druse," said Ethel, sounding friendly again. "But you'll have to go on your own and report back to me. I'm taking some of the first-years for a picnic tomorrow afternoon."

"A picnic!" exclaimed Drusilla. "With a whole lot of first-years?"

"I just thought I'd do a few things to prove how popular I am with the whole school," said Ethel. "You know, just to make sure I'll be chosen as next year's Head Girl."

"*You* don't have to worry about that," said Drusilla admiringly. "You don't have to do anything at all except be a Hallow."

"True." Ethel smiled smugly. "But it won't hurt to do a few extra bits and pieces. Being nice to the first-years will help towards First Prize for Team Spirit, and I've had

the highest grades in everything for the last four years so I'll definitely get First Prize for Highest Grades, and probably First Prize for Best Pilot now that Mildred's had an awful Summer Term with Tabby.

So I'm bound to win everything, plus the nomination for next year's Head Girl. I don't know why the rest of the school is bothering to turn up!" She laughed merrily at her own joke, though Drusilla suspected that Ethel wasn't joking at all.

"I can't think of any prize *I* might get," said Drusilla.

"Cheer up," said Ethel. "There's a prize for keeping your room tidy. You might get that."

"I don't know why they even have a prize for that," mumbled Drusilla. "We've only got a bed and a wardrobe."

A tiny flicker of sympathy flared in Ethel. "Come on, Druse," she said. "We *do* have a good time together—well, *mostly*—don't we? And I just know you'll get some key piece of information about Mildred and those animals tomorrow. I can't wait to find out."

Drusilla's news was better than anything Ethel could have imagined. She had arrived at the circus in time for the evening show, and had seen with increasing astonishment that all the Brilliantines' new acts consisted of an assortment of enchanted brushes, which could only have come from Miss Cackle's Academy—all of which she recounted in great detail to Ethel the moment she arrived back at school.

"This is totally perfect, Druse!" cackled Ethel, grabbing Drusilla and jumping up and down. "Trivial use of magic! Stealing school property! Leaving school without permission! You are an absolutely ace detective! I'd better go and tell Miss Cackle right now before things get any worse."

CHAPTER TWENTY-SEVEN

WHEN ETHEL arrived with her news, Miss Cackle and Miss Hardbroom had been in the process of making a final list of candidates for next year's Head Girl.

"Well, that explains everything," said Miss Cackle with a sigh, closing the door behind Ethel. "I wondered how Mildred had managed it."

"Ethel's right, of course," said Miss Hardbroom. "You can't get more trivial than using magic for a circus act."

"And yet," said Miss Cackle, "it *isn't*

exactly trivial when you consider that Mildred was doing her very best to get her broom companion back again. It must have been hard for her, sending him away when he really didn't want to go. I can't help feeling that if the circus owners are happy with their new display and Mildred can regain her place as one of our best fliers, it does seem that everyone's happy, aren't they? Even little Dulcie."

"Whatever you say, Headmistress," muttered Miss Hardbroom unenthusiastically.

"I must admit," continued Miss Cackle, "Mildred does have a quite extraordinary knack of sorting things out, doesn't she?"

"I suppose that is *one* way of looking at it," sniffed Miss Hardbroom.

"Sometimes I think it is the *only* way of looking at it as far as Mildred is concerned," said Miss Cackle. "I mean, here we are, making lists of all the qualities needed for our Head Girl and, when you *really* think about it, Mildred has the lot."

Miss Hardbroom glanced sharply at Miss Cackle, as she could suddenly see which way this conversation was heading.

"But I thought we had agreed that Ethel was our candidate for Head Girl," she said firmly. "Her marks are always one hundred percent, and of course she is a Hallow, and they are always Head Girl—if there is a Hallow available. A Hallow has been Head Girl for the last two hundred years—it's a proud family tradition. Five minutes ago, Mildred Hubble wasn't in the running at all!"

"I'm not so sure about Ethel," pondered Miss Cackle. "She can be a real sneak sometimes, which, if you think about it, is not exactly a sterling quality—and on one occasion she even stole Mildred's spell and tried to pass it off as her own. You wouldn't

160

catch Mildred Hubble doing something like that, *and* Mildred saved the entire school from my appalling twin sister not once but twice!"

"Both times by accident," said Miss Hardbroom. "That first time, she was actually running away and only stumbled across your sister's coven by chance."

"A happy chance, though," parried Miss Cackle. "If she hadn't been there, we all would have been turned into snails. Then the dear girl saved Mr. Rowan Webb from a lifetime of frogdom in the school pond, and he was so grateful to her that he invited us to stay in his castle for our summer holiday—surely you remember all this, Miss Hardbroom? And, while we were there, Mildred found the lost treasure chest, which paid for all the school roofs to be mended. And that spell I mentioned, the one that Ethel stole, happens to be the best spell ever invented by a pupil in all the time I have been headmistress here.

"And only last term Mildred teamed up with that dear little dog and won the swimming-pool competition — no wonder she wanted him back at any cost! She may have a very exasperating way of doing things, but she does get there in the end — and in the most spectacular way, you must admit, Miss Hardbroom."

"What exactly are you suggesting?" asked Miss Hardbroom.

"I think I'm suggesting," said Miss Cackle, "that it's time for a change."

CHAPTER TWENTY-EIGHT

THE CEREMONY of Fourth-Year Firsts had finally arrived, and the Great Hall echoed with the joyful notes of Miss Bat's piano, playing the customary tune of "In an English Country Garden."

The girls entered the hall, one class at a time, very tightly controlled, as if they might all run amok if Miss Hardbroom's beady eye was taken off them for one second—which was ridiculous really, as they were all wearing their best robes and were on their very best behaviour to match. They shuffled along the rows of chairs, arranging themselves as neatly as possible, with Year One at the front, followed by Year Two behind them, and so on, with Year Four at the back. Year Five sat on the stage, behind the teachers.

There would be countless awards, cups, medals, prizes, and certificates given out, plus lengthy speeches and accolades to the Year Fives, who would be leaving the school on that very day, and Miss Cackle would be droning on for hours. Mildred had little hope for a Fourth-Year First in anything, so she had brought a mini book of crosswords and a pencil to surreptitiously pass the time. It was helpful that they were in the back row, with several rows of pupils blocking the view from the stage.

"Let's wait and see if Maud gets First Prize for Team Spirit," said Mildred to Enid, "then we can get stuck into these crosswords. I can do one, then pass the book to you, and we can see who finishes the most. It's going to be a bit boring otherwise,

just sitting here for hours, watching Ethel get every prize in the universe."

"Hey!" said Enid. "I might actually win something."

"Like what?" asked Mildred as they both dissolved into giggles.

"You never know," said Enid. "They might invent a new category just for me!"

"Quieten down in the back row!" barked Miss Hardbroom. "Things are getting a little raucous!"

Mildred and Enid stopped whispering and immediately sat bolt upright.

At last, the entire school was crammed into the Great Hall, the final notes of the piano died away, and the speeches began. Miss Hardbroom was first, congratulating the departing Year Fives on all their hard work and wishing them luck with the results of their Witches' Higher Certificate exams, which they would not receive for several months. Mildred had always thought that this was an excellent system, as no one would know if she had failed until they had all left the school.

Maud had laughed when Mildred pointed this out. "You're such a pessimist, Millie," she'd said. "I mean, you might do really well, then you'll miss out on all the praise *and* Ethel seething. It's always seemed odd to me that we'll all leave without knowing if we passed or not."

"And now," continued Miss Cackle, taking over cheerfully from Miss Hardbroom, "to our first award of this most important day. The First Prize for Highest Grades over the last four years goes to . . . Ethel Hallow! No surprise there!"

She smiled, beckoning to Ethel, who barged along the row of seated pupils, sending cats flying as she hurried to claim her trophy, a huge wooden-and-silver shield with Ethel's name neatly inscribed beneath last year's winner.

No sooner had Ethel sat down than she was called up again, this time to take First Prize for Best Pilot: a beautiful cup with handles shaped like broomsticks. Drusilla clapped loudly, and the rest of the school clapped too, but without the burst of spontaneous delight that sometimes erupts at such a prize-giving.

"Of course there have been other excellent fliers recently," said Miss Cackle, "and many pupils who have improved considerably, but these Firsts are for consistent work since day one, so another big 'well done' to Ethel Hallow."

Ethel beamed from ear to ear, looking unbearably smug.

"This is going to be a wipeout," muttered Enid.

CHAPTER TWENTY-NINE

IN FACT, it wasn't a total wipeout. To everyone's delight, Maud won First Prize for Team Spirit.

This prize was voted for by the girls themselves, so Maud won hands down, as she was genuinely helpful, always spending time with the younger pupils, and on the lookout for team-spirited activities, such as tidying the broom shed and gathering up litter. The first-years had seen through Ethel's last-minute efforts, and everyone in the school (except Drusilla and Sybil, Ethel's younger sister) had voted for Maud.

A huge cheer burst out when Maud clumped up to the stage, beaming from ear to ear, to collect her prize, a gigantic silver urn, which was almost as big as herself.

The cheers died away, and Maud struggled back to her seat and rearranged herself, almost hidden by the trophy on her lap.

"Oh, Maudie!" said Mildred, who was immensely proud of her friend. "I'm so

glad you won it. Now we can all go home happy."

"Congrats, Maud," agreed Enid. "That's *some* trophy! You'll need an extra room to keep it in!"

"Settle down back there!" said Miss Hardbroom, rising ominously from her chair and peering in their direction. Everyone dropped their eyes obediently.

Next, Miss Cackle began her tribute to the Year Fives, going on at length about how much they would all be missed and wishing them luck for the future. As usual, most of the leavers were in floods of tears.

"Why on earth do they always cry?" whispered Mildred, ducking conveniently behind Maud's trophy.

"It's weird, isn't it?" replied Maud. "The Year Fives always cry on the last day. I suppose we will too."

"I won't!" whispered Enid.

Maud put a finger to her lips, anxious not to draw attention to herself now that the much-wanted Team Spirit trophy was in her clutches.

The ceremony dragged on. Speeches were made to the departing pupils by all the teachers, including Miss Bat, who kept forgetting what she was saying, so it took twice as long. More first prizes were awarded to the Year Fours, mainly won by Ethel, who was now sitting at the end of the row, so that she could pile up the cups and shields.

Mildred and Enid had given up hoping for a prize. The only ones in their range were non-academic ones such as First Prize for the Tidiest Room or First Prize for the Best-Trained Cat. Unfortunately, the whole school knew about Mildred's troubles with Tabby, as well as Enid's monkey episode, and they were both renowned for their inability to keep their belongings tidy.

Mildred had already opened the book of crosswords, keeping it out of sight on her lap. The first one had been easy; she'd finished it in ten minutes, then passed it sideways to Enid. Twenty minutes later, Enid completed the second one and passed it back, taking great care not to be seen.

At first, Mildred kept glancing up at the stage while she was trying to solve the clues, in case anyone noticed that she wasn't paying attention, but the third crossword was much more difficult than the first. This one was full of references to books or plays containing magic objects, and Mildred became so engrossed in it that the background noises of speeches and applause faded away until she was no longer aware of them.

She had only managed to answer three clues before she got completely stuck on 4 down: *To whom did the Lady of the Lake give the Ring of Dispel? (Two words: 3, 8.)*

This is really hard, Mildred thought to herself, racking her brain. *I know! The Lady of the Lake gave Excalibur to King Arthur* —that's *two words! Maybe she gave him the ring too! No, hang on* —*the first word has only three letters, and there are four letters in "king." I wonder if* —

"Stand up, Mildred Hubble!" Miss Hardbroom's voice rang out across the rows of silent pupils.

CHAPTER THIRTY

H ORRIFIED, Mildred leapt to
her feet.
    "I — er — um — I'm . . ."
she spluttered.
    "Surprised?" said Miss Cackle, smiling
warmly. "You were miles away, weren't
you, my dear?"

Confused, Mildred realized that Meredith Frost, the outgoing Head Girl, was standing between Miss Cackle and Miss Hardbroom, unpinning the Head-Girl medal from the front of her robe.

"Come along, Mildred," said Miss Cackle encouragingly. "Up you come. We're all waiting for you!"

Mildred glanced at Maud, still half-hidden behind her Team Spirit trophy, then at Enid. Her two friends looked astounded, and at the end of the next row, Ethel had turned to glare at her.

"Perhaps you didn't hear at the back there!" said Miss Cackle, now beckoning to Mildred with both arms. "Mildred Hubble, you have been chosen to take over from Meredith as next year's Head Girl!"

Mildred looked around in shock as the whole school erupted in cheers of delight—well, *almost* the whole school. Ethel was also in shock, her mouth open in astonishment as she realized that she would be the first Hallow in two hundred years not to be Head Girl. Mildred couldn't help feeling sorry for her archenemy as she made her way through the joyful throng and bounded up the steps to receive the medal, swept up on a wave of total happiness.

Miss Cackle put her arms around Meredith and Mildred. "You can't wear it yet!" She laughed as she saw that Mildred was attempting to attach the medal to her robe.

"Sorry, Miss Cackle," gasped Mildred. "I got a bit carried away!"

"Just keep it safe," said Miss Cackle. "Ready for next year."

"Or we could keep it for you here, Mildred," suggested Miss Hardbroom. "In case you lose it."

"I don't think that will be necessary, Miss Hardbroom," said Miss Cackle. "One of the reasons why we chose Mildred as Head Girl, if you remember, is her ability to learn from her mistakes over the last four years, and to become stronger and more reliable as a result—an excellent role model for the younger girls, don't you think?"

"Hmmmm," muttered Miss Hardbroom. "Simmer down now, girls!" she continued waspishly. "We can see that you're all *overjoyed* with our choice of Head Girl, but that's quite enough silly nonsense for now."

Gradually, the noise died down. Meredith returned to her seat with a kindly squeeze of Mildred's shoulder, and Mildred slipped the treasured medal into her pocket and turned to the steps.

"Wait a moment, my dear," said Miss Cackle. "Don't forget. You must choose your deputy—Head Girl's privilege!"

"May I choose anybody?" asked Mildred.

179

"Of course," said Miss Cackle. "It's absolutely your choice."

"So choose wisely, Mildred," sniped Miss Hardbroom.

Mildred looked around the sea of pupils — Ethel buzzing with rage and various friends looking up at her hopefully, giving little waves or pointing at themselves, mouthing, *Pleease!*

Mildred's gaze came to rest on Enid, who was smiling madly, eyes like saucers, and Maud, who was craning her head above the Team Spirit trophy, pointing at Enid and nodding.

"I'd like Enid as my deputy, Miss Cackle," said Mildred solemnly. "Would that be all right?"

CHAPTER THIRTY-ONE

THE THREE friends were on the way back to their rooms; it was taking forever, as Mildred and Enid were stopped by friends every five minutes to show off their medals, and Maud had to keep putting down the heavy Team Spirit trophy to rest her arms.

"I don't know how I'm going to get it on the broom," she said. "I've got too much luggage already."

"Don't worry," said Mildred helpfully. "You can tie it on. I've got a big laundry bag that I could lend you—you can pack clothes round it so it won't get scratched."

"That's our new Head Girl," said Enid, "sorting out all our problems. Thanks for choosing me as your deputy, Millie. I wasn't expecting anything at all."

"Isn't it brilliant?" Maud laughed, picking up her trophy and tottering up the corridor. "All three of us covered in glory! Who would have thought it?"

"Certainly not me!" said Miss Hardbroom's chilly voice as she appeared, literally, in a dark doorway ahead of them. The girls stopped in their tracks. "Quite the little game-changer, aren't you, Mildred Hubble? Dogs on broomsticks and a non-Hallow as Head Girl—whatever next? I only hope that you will work hard next year and live up to this challenge."

"Oh, I *will*, Miss Hardbroom," said Mildred sincerely. "I'll do my very best to set an example to the lower school. I won't let you down—I promise on my honour."

Miss Hardbroom peered at them silently for a few moments, noting how petrified they all looked—even Star, now cowering behind Enid's ankles—and she found herself wishing that the girls weren't *quite* so terrified of her *all* the time.

"Now, girls," she said suddenly, a tiny smile flickering for a brief second. "I forgot to say a resounding 'Well done!' to all three of you!"

"Thank you, Miss Hardbroom," chorused the girls, not quite sure what to do next.

"Well, off you go, then," said Miss Hardbroom, whose kindly mood had lasted precisely thirty seconds. "Oh, just one more thing, Mildred."

Mildred froze.

"The answer to four down in your crossword puzzle?" continued Miss Hardbroom. "It's Sir Lancelot — I thought you might like to know."

"Thank you, Miss Hardbroom," mumbled Mildred.

"Well, you'd better collect your belongings and get down to the playground for end-of-term takeoff!" announced Miss Hardbroom. "Happy holidays, girls — and take care of that medal, Mildred!" So saying, she vanished abruptly.

184

The three friends waited in silence for several minutes, as H.B. sometimes lurked, invisible, to catch them out.

"That's it!" said Mildred. "The air's warmed up—she's gone! Come on, let's get out of here—"

"Before anything goes wrong!" said Enid.

"I'm sure it won't," declared Maud. "Anyway, I'm just pleased we all got what we wanted."

"Even me!" announced Mildred happily. "*Just* what I wanted—First Prize for the Worst Witch!"